ANTHONY BROWNE

FRIDA AND BEAR

HANNE BARTHOLIN

Frida loved to draw.

First published in the UK in 2015 by Walker Books Ltd
87 Vauxhall Walk, London SE11 5HJ

2 4 6 8 10 9 7 5 3 1

© 2015 Brun Limited & Hanne Bartholin

The right of Anthony Browne and Hanne Bartholin to be identified as authors and illustrators of this work
has been asserted by them in accordance with the Copyright, Designs and Patents Act 1988

This book has been typeset in Futura

Printed in China

British Library Cataloguing in Publication Data:
a catalogue record for this book is available from the British Library

ISBN 978-1-4063-5399-0

www.walker.co.uk

WALKER BOOKS
AND SUBSIDIARIES
LONDON • BOSTON • SYDNEY • AUCKLAND

And so did Bear.
But one day Bear couldn't think of anything to draw.
"What can I draw, Frida?" he said.

Frida drew a shape,
and gave it to Bear.

"Try and turn this shape into something, Bear,"
said Frida.

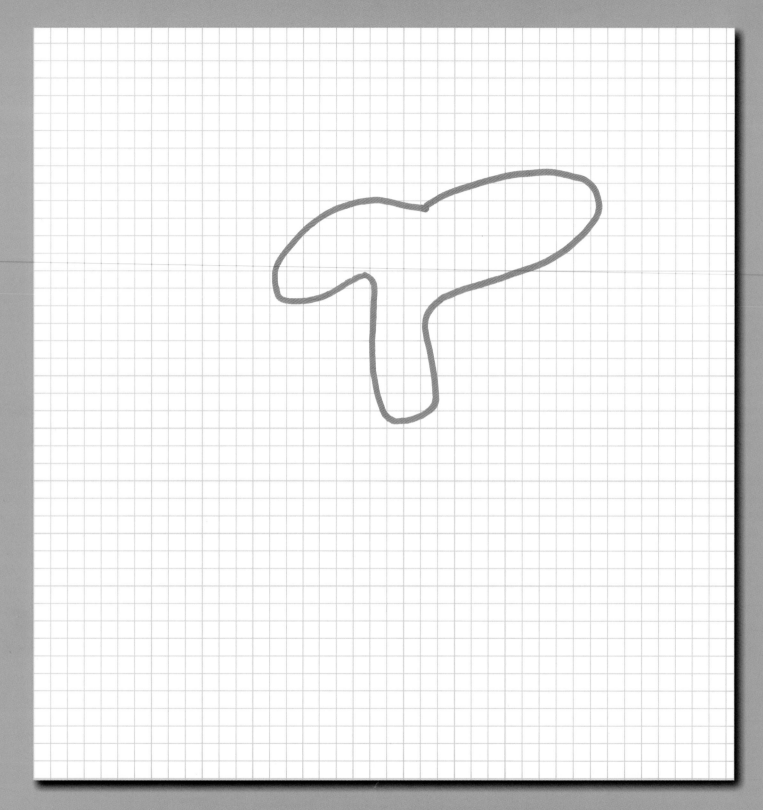

Bear looked at the shape ... and started to draw.

He turned the shape into a puppy.

"It's my turn now, Frida," said Bear.

So he drew a shape, and passed it to Frida.

Frida turned it into a fish.

"Oooh, that's a **big** fish!" said Bear.

It was Frida's turn, so again,
she drew a shape for Bear.

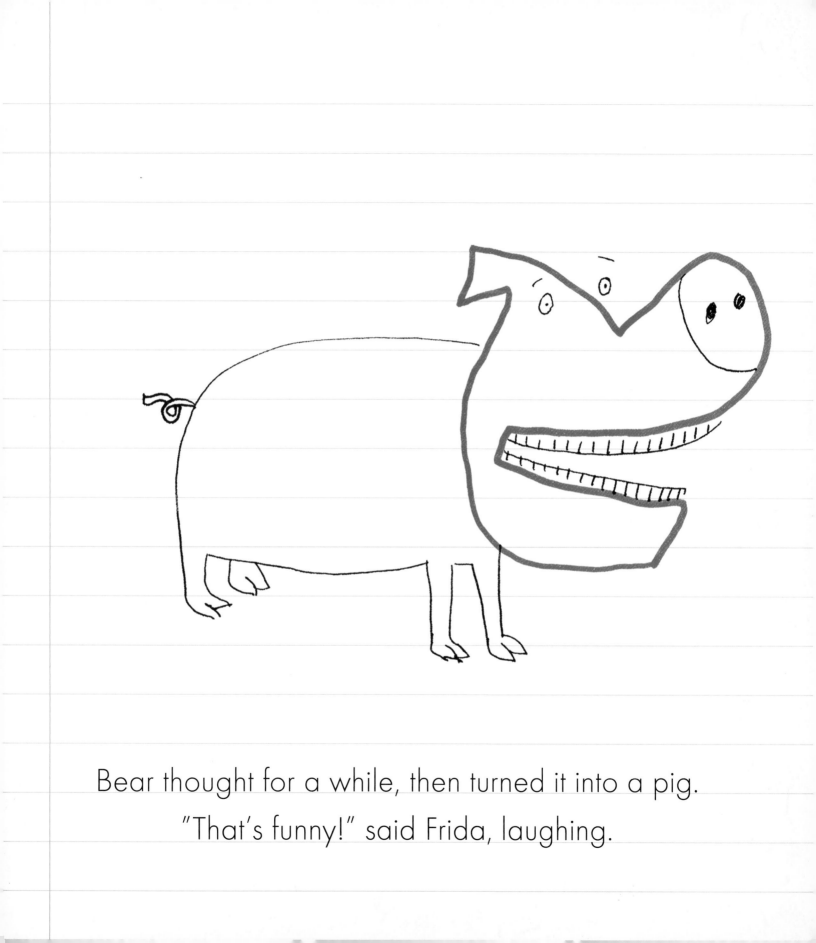

Bear thought for a while, then turned it into a pig.
"That's funny!" said Frida, laughing.

Bear made another shape...

Frida turned it into a funny little man.

Frida gave Bear a piece of wrapping paper.

"I know what that looks like," said Bear,
and he began to draw.

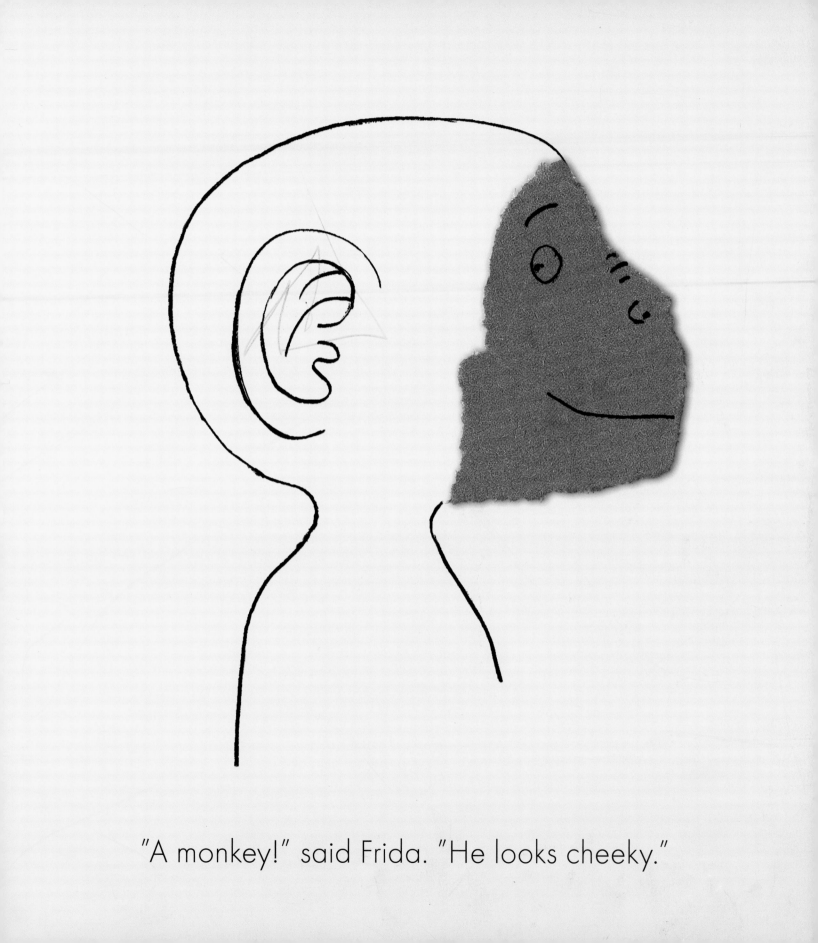

"A monkey!" said Frida. "He looks cheeky."

Bear took a twig out of his pocket
and gave it to Frida.
"I wonder what that could be?" said Frida.
"Ah, I know!"

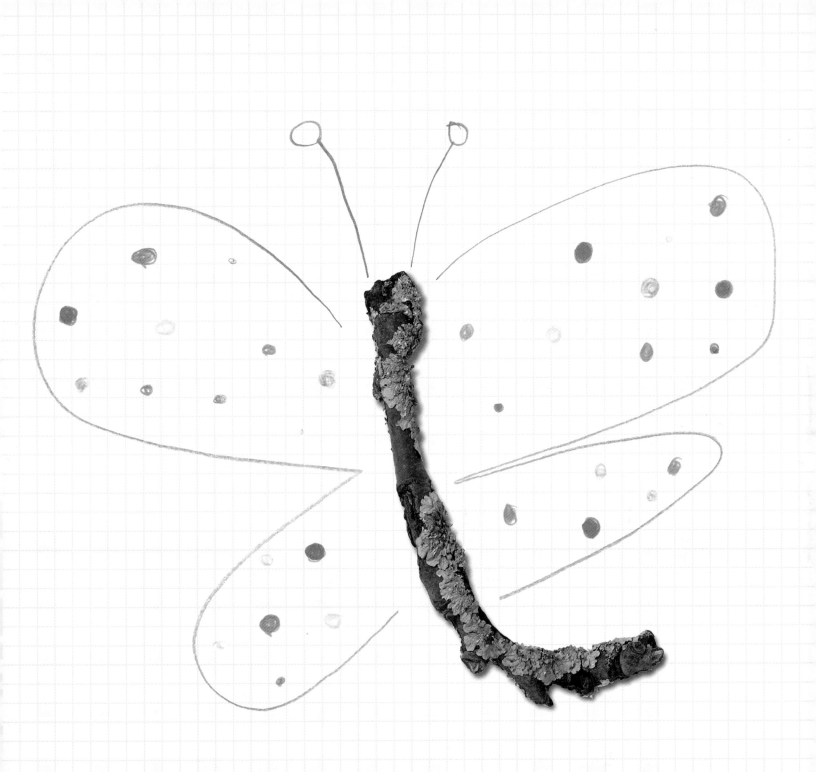

And Frida turned it into a butterfly.
"That's lovely!" said Bear. "Well done."

Frida and Bear love this game

and play it every day.

Look at all the pictures Frida and Bear
have drawn!

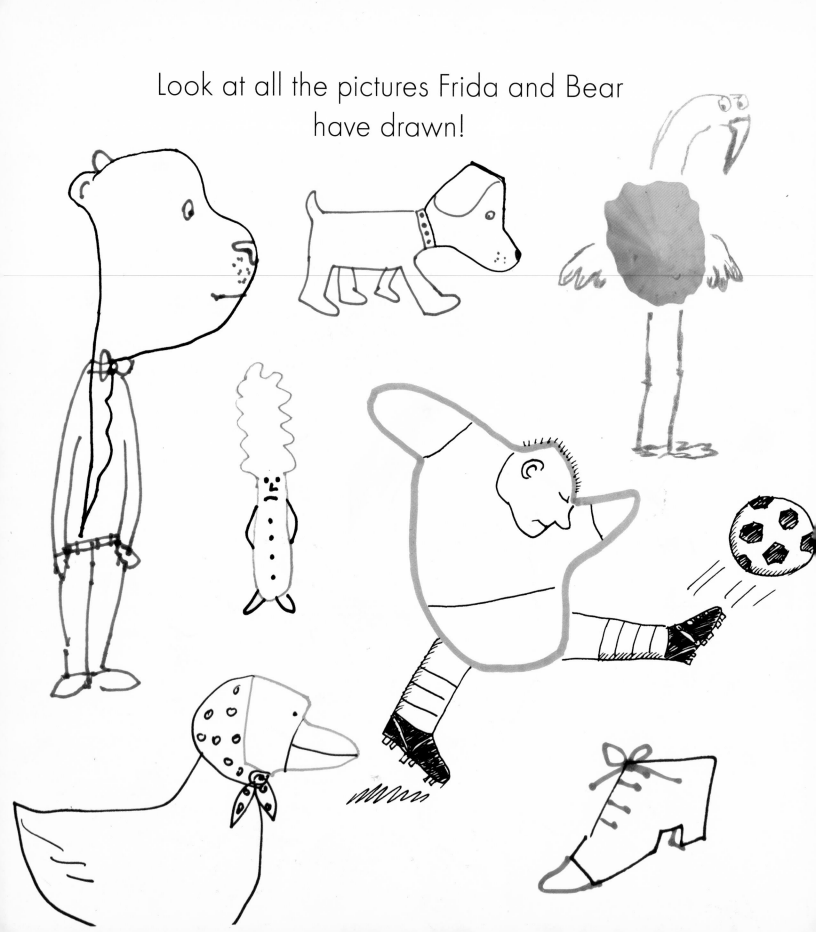

Why don't you draw some
shapes and play?